POETRY:
NOT OPTIONAL

Poems by

LISA
MOONCAT

DOCKYARD PRESS

Poetry: Not Optional

ISBN 978-1-913452-60-5

Contents

Childhood

The Journey

Sex

Love

Family

POETRY: NOT OPTIONAL

Childhood

THE FIRST POEM

I sit confused,
lost for thought,
trying to flee,
from fears distraught,
the feeling alone,
echoes far, far away,
as if in a desert,
in the back of my head,
as I lay in bed.

7/6/1994
Diary

LOST

I am lost,
in a world where nothing makes sense to me.
I am lost,
carried across the sea.
I am lost,
in a waltz of the flowers.
I am lost,
in a dance of the hours.
I am lost,
in a dark wood.
I am lost,
in a storm without a hood.
I am lost,
left out here to die.
I am lost,
so under the stars I lie.
I am lost,
torn up on the waves.
I am lost,
in a cold shimmery grave.

5/15/1996
The First Journal

LOVE

Love will see you through a day,
gloomy still and dark.
Love will thrive in a day,
when birds live and lark.
Love is a guard at a castle,
in a magic enchanted world.
Love is a guide in a wood,
with trails that weave and curl.
Love will sail you in a boat,
far across the sea.
Love will see you through it all.
Love is you and me.

6/4/1996
The First Journal

THIS WORLD

A place to be,
a place that's mine.
Away from the rush,
of people and time.
In my world,
all alone.
I am not lost,
for there's nowhere to go.
Trapped in the gray,
between black and white.
I see the difference,
between dark and light.
Opposites attract,
so they say.
But when they clash,
who will pay.
People fear,
what they don't understand.
Yet they resist knowledge,
of Mother Nature's plan.
Confused and dazed,
I come across.
Though it seems,
I'm not really lost.

1/10/1997
The Smile

FOOTSTEPS

Footsteps running, running, running,
louder and louder it grows.
Footsteps running, running, running,
I see the traveler, there he goes.
Footsteps running, dimming, running,
to pass me by he chose.
Footsteps dimming, running, dimming,
going where? No one knows.

3/23/1997
The Smile

IN BETWEEN

A single tear
a feather on the dry
on the surface of my skin
forbidden to cry.
My mind screams help!
My stomachs in a knot.
My heart is in turmoil,
my eyes are burning hot.
I'm helpless and confused,
pain from my own condition
wishing hell upon myself,
upon my own expression.
Thoughts are few and fleeting
and dreams altogether absurd.
My mind destroys my heart
and my heart destroys my courage.
My conscience is unknown to me,
and it hurts to look around,
at all the fear and hurt,
it's all I've ever found.
Some things are made for wishes
and some things are made for dreams.
But I myself am nothing,
I am the in between.

8/7/1997
The Art Book

15

TRY

look into my eyes
touch my hand.
see the hurt,
understand.
next time you
see a child
a child who
is scared
not of something material,
of something like love,
that isn't there.
remember me.
when you touched my hand,
reach out
understand.

10/4/1997
Poems and Songs

17

LOOK #1

smile, look down
question, look around
statement, look here
suspicion, look there
remember, look back
exclamation, look at that
old fashioned, a look see
love, look at me

LOOK #2

look here
look there
look everywhere
look down
look around
stop

don't think
don't speak
don't say a word
never thought
never said
never heard

question ask
think aloud
do not see
time pass
not a sound
never be

LOOK #3

It's never the same on both sides of the sky
It's never the same on both sides of my eyes
When I look around I don't see what you see
When you look around you don't see me.

12/18/1997
Poems and Songs

THE QUESTION

You know,
but you don't,
the question
stays afloat.
What do you do
when you're wrong?
Do you go?
Do you stay?
You still
walk away.
Go your own way,
or follow along?

12/18/1997
Poems and Songs

SUNBEAM

Walk the trees
drink the sky
watch the world
as it flies by.
Taste the air
feel the dirt
see the life
spring from the earth.
Talk to the shadows
follow the stream
live inside
a sunbeam.

7/23/1998 Thursday
The Project Notebook

SUNRISE

Sunrise on a summer morn so peaceful and serene.
Here I am, all alone to greet the dawning day.
Sunrise ease my troubled mind of all I've done and
      seen,
keep me everlasting in your soft and peaceful ways.
Troubled is this heart of mine that knows so much of
      pain.
Fallen is this world of mine from love to such
      despair.
All I keep on hearing is the falling of the rain,
to the beating of my heart, I hate this quiet pair.
Sunrise clears all sound from me and soothes my
      mournful heart.
Here I sit regarding just the sunrise in its splendor.
As I sit here in such awe, I know I must depart.
Ever in my heart will stay the love the sunrise
      rendered.

8/6/1998 Thursday
The Project Notebook

*

I fall through the shadows all around me,
I touch nothing except the cool darkness.
I feel as though I am made of air,
I feel like sunlight, golden mesh.
Walk through the forest and look around.
My body touches all that you see.
I am nowhere all at once,
but everywhere is me.
At night I am the smoke,
dancing towards the sky.
The moonlight shows me here
as I dance all through the night.
Then I become the dew,
greeting the scarlet dawn.
It sparkles through my being
until I am gone.

8/16/1998 Sunday
The Project Notebook

27

DAYLIGHT

I am walking the
winds of fate,
looking out
across my destiny.
I sit now at the
crossroads of time,
the river that flows
out to the sea.
I am a traveler
weary and old,
I know this road
like no other.
I age not
in this place,
for I bathe each day
in time's ever flowing river.
Then I don my traveler's cloak
and once again start on my way,
to follow the sun in its course,
in the ever aging day.

8/24/1998
The Split

STARS

At the end of every day
Remember where you are
Look up at the sky
Sparkling with stars.
Know inside your heart
You are always free to dream
The stars are not as far
As they may seem.

10/26/1998
Blue

ONE DAY ANEW

Here I sit
crossed in thought
walking the paths
I should have walked
contemplating
this dying day
in my own
peaceful way
I think on all the things I've done.
Things I've finished or begun.
All the things I wanted to do
and tomorrow I will start anew
knowing I failed yesterday's trials
and ready to face them with a smile.

2/18/1999
Spikey

SHADOW MEMORY

Shadows pace in circles
they trace the paths I've walked
they hide inside my dreams
and they linger in my thoughts.
I try to shake them loose
in order to see more clearly,
but there is no escaping their grasp,
they're hiding myself from my memory.
Inside those memories they arise
showing their sweet solid black
making holes in the stories I know
forbidding me now, to look back.
The picture show starts in my head
with the shadows playing their part
they're hiding what I want to know
they're pulling my memory apart.

8/1/2000
The Halfway

THE SCREAMER

A witness to the burning tears
of her rising scream,
I stop and think.
She opens her mouth to release that piercing cry
at the slightest provocation.
But unlike some, my ears have not
grown deaf to her call.
I still hear it.
She is so ignorant and selfish
screaming only for herself,
but I respond.
And I don't know how to curtail
myself and be mature,
I am not strong enough.
I try to be reasonable and thoughtful
and think of other people,
but I always give in.
I hate it, that screamer,
that crying, malicious, bitch,
but she is inside of me.
I've tried for years to escape
and repress her,
but in the end I return.
Then I wonder.
Is that the real me,
because I try not to be her,
but she always comes back.

Do I hate myself?
Say no. Please. Say no.

8/31/2000
High School Summer

WAKING

And the sun will set with a western blaze
and blow your sleeping mind away.
When you wake you'll find your blood
spilling out to join the flood.
As all around you cannot hear
your waking cries fall on deaf ears.
The noise of life is deafening
to one who's new to the throbbing ring.
You long to go to your former state.
Wake up, it's too late.

10/16/2000
High School Summer

39

The Journey

LUCKY GIRL

I feel as though I've reached an end,
a point where everything starts again,
like a part of me has died and gone,
and in its place something new is going on.
I am seeing what I never saw before.
Everywhere, inside and outside, is more.
Now I can taste more in one bite
than I tasted before in all of my life.
And everything looks so fresh and new,
but weathered and old and respected too.
All of the people are different somehow,
they seem so alone when I look at them now.
I just want to reach out and touch everyone,
and let everyone know they are special and loved.
But these people do not need that from me.
I think maybe I want them to touch me.
Like a baby again, that has just been born,
I want to be loved and safe and warm.
But I feel the rush of the world alone.
Walking around in the world on my own.
Yes, here I am, starting all over,
but I know in my pocket there's a four leaf clover.

6/30/2001
The Travel Book

43

TRAVELER

Stars twinkle above my head
as I walk alone at night.
Their light will keep my spirit fed
and still my beating heart from fright.
I'm still alive! I think out loud
even though not a soul can hear me.
With every step I stand tall and proud
I walk so well here, no creature will fear me.
But this is not an ambling gait
each stride brings me closer to my goal.
I've not lost patience, but I cannot wait.
The Moon has said that I must go.
She lights the path beneath my feet,
my heart knows not my destination.
The travelers home becomes the street.
I want not to have a home, or make one.
Without a home I'm truly free,
happy to wander on my own.
I answer to none but the Goddess and me,
the stars, the Moon and the open road.

3/17/2003
The Stowaway

THE WAY

As each day I grow
I define myself again
Trying, I reach for parameters
that I will ultimately bend
to shape ideas
as I use them.
My own free will
re-explaining destiny.
Each step of the way
saved by those who've gone before,
but not the same distance!
This path is different,
never better, bolder.
I go.

7/31/2008
Loose Leaf

IN THE GRIT

Standing on the platform.
Contemplating time
as a general notion
a potent antidote
to the stillness
to rest
a blessing in disgust
maintaining a base frequency
adding to the intensity
adrift on the sea of particles
causing space for creation
wading through the mire
inspired
but tired
of waiting.

10/25/2010
The Night Pages

TODAY IS ANY DAY

I went to Trabubuland,
I talked to the VooDoo man,
I sang with the mockingbirds,
I tell the tale of what I heard.
That big round sound
from deep underground,
came rolling up to meet the sea
and on the way encountered me.
So I set sail,
with the wind on my tail,
on my brother's boat,
with a dream I wrote.
How much I loved you
but a love so unpure,
full of funny situations,
full of sums without equations.
Innocence is lost
cost me my idealism.
Wisdom came to visit that day,
he got lost along the way,
but I understood.
There's a dark scary wood
and a long winding drive
on the other side.
You have to cross that
to get here.
Have no fear.

Spit back
at the wolves that encircle you.

8/7/2006
The Occidental

CHANGE

rearranges
in a strange way
my day.
Master plan,
faster than
superman
quadruple span
the effects
of sweat.
Of work in the dirt
of life's trifles
stifling
my ability to see.
To let be the new me.
Inside
my mind
is new
but you
won't recognize
my new life.
From this side
of my eyes
it's clear.
It's here.
It's come.
It's done.
Step one,

begun!
But not finished
it's just the beginning.
Soul replenished.
Step two
I explain to you
how through
this experience
of making sense
from scattered thoughts
I'm caught.
In a new reality.
Awake from dreaming.
Like a light turned on.
Dawn.

12/5/2003
The Student

FREE FLOW JUMP

At what point did I stop trying to understand?
I'm now, honestly, just trying to be.
Accepting the things that are out of my hands,
willing myself to let Love flow freely.
There's always more love to give and to share,
as long as I'm open to the Love that's there.
The easier it comes and goes
the closer I am to the Path of true flow.
Acknowledging the new direction of life's changes.
Doing my best to learn as it rearranges.
Growing again with each new situation,
sometimes without time for contemplation.
Being ready to jump
the net will appear.
The only thing holding you back from your Truth
is your Fear.

4/11/11
Walls

DIG IN

The rain came
and pushed me under cover
of a café
attempting to eat pastries with a fork.
I recognize the futility
after one bite
put down this questionable utensil
and dig in.
Frosting under my nails,
powdered sugar
on my black dress.
I surrender to
decadence.

10/27/2010
The Night Pages

JUDGEMENT

I am not what you were expecting.
This is my experience
with second guessing
drifting through your weariness.
I'm trying to explain
as best I can to you
my current fears and pain
what I'm going through.
In just as many words
I trust what I've heard.
For no good reason
my soul stands treason
at other people's trial
of my worthwhile.

11/22/2003
The Student

FAITH

Perception
receiving
those believing
even after a second guess.
Oppressed
soul undressed
plagued by this strip show of my faith.
I wait
caught
in my thoughts
wishing for reality
to appear to me
make clear this muddy sea
of illusions
that surround my conclusions
gone unsaid
just in my head
in bed
having sex
with my personal politics.
Are my ideas pure?
It remains unsure.
What the old men wrote
was a joke to me.
I hope to be free
one day
from the things they say.

6/5/2004
The Pod

LET ME BE SOFT

I remember
the way things were
in those days
in a way
that I can't explain.
I refrain
and it tortures
my heart,
no closure,
torn apart.
I love unconditionally
unjudgementally.
I try to be pleasing,
but it never is enough.
Not for you,
I'm not that tough,
it's true.
I have something else to offer.
I am softer.
To love me
fully,
you must understand
that I try to accept every woman and man
how they are.
I find them so hard.
Harder than the grindstone.
I do not live that tone.

They come to me
because I am changing,
and I let them change too.
But you,
don't let me change,
because you think it's not necessary.
I must rearrange
as does my reality.
My life is soft, as am I.
This is not me living a lie.
Understand me, or please just try.

2/15/2005
The Pod

*

Life
sometimes
winds
beyond your own eyes
expect
the worst
of intellects curse
damaging you
with every move
every idea is a credo
moving you closer to evil
let your mind go
let your heart lead
and each beat
will bring you closer to love.

11/26/2006
Back in the USA

GENERATION GAP

I get so angry
when you can't understand me.
Inevitable,
it's not your fault
or mine
it's just time,
different lines
for the coloring.
Smothering.
I forgot and I let those lines
define not just me,
but my whole reality.
Yours is so different.
As sentient
and engaged as I could be
I will not see
nor will you.
It's related
but not the same.

2/14/2005
The Pod

TRUTH AS CLEAR TO ANYONE

Clarity
and understanding
go hand in hand,
I guess
by who's demand?
What a mess.
With religion
and freedom
and governmental unrest,
we pit brothers
against one another
and you know all the rest.
The warfare,
the bloodshed,
the blank stares
from hearts of lead.
And we all say we know,
but obviously we don't.
One thing
seems
clear to me,
the argument swings
and now it's clear to you.
Who
I ask you.
Who knows the Truth?

2/15/2005
The Pod

SILT

The line
in my mind
defined
at one point in time
has now become blurred
stirred up
like silt
from the bottom of the river.

2/19/2020 Wednesday
Tiger Stripes and Leopard Spots

NIGHTMARE

Turbulent dream schemes
wake me
nightly
toying with time
destroying peace of mind
the fable
disabled
I cannot run
from the fears I've spun
anymore
I contort
my psyche.

8/31/2004
The Pod

THE MACHINE

When do we give in to humanity's machine?
At what point does it become part of the dream?
From the back of our mind's eyes we stop trying to
    see
and close our hearts to the idea of being free.
All dried up until we can't even bleed.

How do we maintain our visions of Love?
And work the machine towards what WE dream of?
Without getting caught up
or burnt out
or feeling broken and lost
in a sea of the blindly devout.

I promise to remember my dream
and make the machine work for me!

5/5/2011
Walls

HELL

Oh mediocrity
where did you come from?
Go Away!
Back to the place you were spun.
In this beautiful tapestry of life
how has your thread come so close to mine?
I wanted to be a Rockstar,
not an English teacher!
I guess my path
is one less featured.
I'm a simple creature.
Habitual I am not.
This lot in life
seems unworthy of my time,
yet here I am,
mundane, the same,
as all those people I said I'd never be.
Wasting
tasting only the most bland.
For what?
Mediocrity.

3/27/2006
The Occidental

*

And the evening comes on
with a peach sky
and the workers all escape their boxes
for another night.
I watch the lamp post
creeping towards my window
like a ghost.
I want to know.
Why?
What one more day
in the game
will accomplish.
If we're not just racing ourselves to the next high
then where are we all going
at 60 miles per hour.
Will it really matter when we get there?
Is it just an illusion
to perpetuate wealth
to force an external will on the Self?
But you can't stop now
you've almost won.
It's a new lie for you.
This time they'll even let you hold the gun.

2/18/2010
The Night Pages

COLD FEET

Waiting again.
We build rooms just for...
Waiting again,
in a line in the downpour.
Waiting again.
Where is that bus at?
Waiting again.
Good thing I brought my hat.

6/12/2006
Back in the USA

FRIDAY NIGHT

I'm so tired
but I haven't done any real work
no soil to toil in
no back breaking dirt.
My nails are clean
but chewed down to the quick
staring into problems for hours
the eyeball stress drip.
Until it all just blurs
into a dream of busyness
until I hit the switch and close the doors
and release my consciousness
to consider its own ideas
and revel in ridiculosity.
I let my mind run free
and instead of overflowing, I find it empty.
After leasing my noticing
for an entire week's work
my creativity is all dried up
too tired to flirt.
Even sexy ideas are not enough
to get me to engage.
My Friday night is lonely and dry
staring at the blank page.

8/5/2011
Walls

STUCK

Like raindrops streaking horizontally on the bus
     window
I fast motion fall into sadness.
Angry like a melted lollipop
now frozen to the window sill
unable to let go, glued in place
after its molten moment passed.
Flapping my gums,
tripping over my tongue
like the 3 year old who left it there to melt
once he lost interest.
I search for the source of my unhappiness
hoping there's a simple solution
knowing it's never as easy as all that.
It can take years for the sun to melt away
the hardened sticky mess.

5/5/2011
Walls

WAR

Here we are the soldiers
of our non-existent culture
looking out to see
what we hope will be
but instead we all see war
human nature's whore
paid by whoever will pay her
for unfulfilling pleasure
she kills all that I love
no chance for the peace I dream of.
I turn my head and cry.
I will no longer fight.

6/6/2003
The Stowaway

ARMAGEDDON IN AMERICA

The forests burned.
Children were caged and died.
Whole cities are sick from polluted rivers.
Islands of trash coalesce on the ocean.
Women are jailed for being raped.

Rich Christian men laugh
and get richer.
Rapists and bigots rage on
in the name of Jesus.

Victims are persecuted.
Mothers are jailed.
Families starve.
Sick people die.

Where is your God now?

for my Christian friends

7/23/2019
Emails

DEEP IN THE NIGHT

Under the stars
my sore heart
throbs again.
When does it end?
I hear time heals
in friendly appeals.
Ask me to smile
just for a while,
but it hurts to start over.
No more four leaf clovers
for this girl.
This world
has cracked open wide,
with a Truth I can't hide,
and it kills me inside.
Searching for peace.
Begging for release
from the cycle.

12/3/2008
Unfinished

THE BEAST

Yellow eyes gleam in the darkness.
Heavy breathing, panting, hunger
drips from her teeth.
I barely see her,
her fur so black,
until her tail swishes and she creeps closer.
She's coming for me.
She always is.
There is no Moon here,
no stars to guide me,
no glitter pathway between the tall trees.
Just us.
On the edge of consciousness.
Where the Dreaming meets the Soul Path.
I confront my fiercest adversary,
myself.

7/3/2020
Tiger Stripes and Leopard Spots

SUICIDE

good enough
spend so much time worrying about
being bad
rebel without reason
the fault
is always mine
senseless
just to feel nothing
escape
to be nowhere
judgement
cannot escape myself

9/8/2013
Butterfly

DON'T JUMP

Sometimes the edge
of your ledge
is not so far
from where you are
and I
can only try
to help
yourself
get back
intact
once you fall.
I saw it all.
I know
how it goes.
I've been there
in despair,
no light,
no sight
in the darkness
of night's kiss.
You're frightless
and solemn.
The bottom
of your bottle
is not full.
It's empty
and angry

like you feel.
It's not real.
It's alive
in your mind.
You keep it
and steep in it
till you're pickled
like a sick old
bastard!
I ask you!
You want this?
You call this bliss?

You can't get past
the last
task
that you failed.
You bailed
at the last minute.
You begin it
but don't finish.
That's a problem.
It's not them.
It's you.
Make your own truth.
I have mine
but I can't find
for someone else
a Self.
A feeling of complete
that's concrete.
It's your turn
and you will get burned.
But at the end

we are still friends.
It's ok
to say
you don't know how to play.
You'll learn.
Court adjourned.
There is no judge
and no jury,
just your fury
to contain.
I know the pain.
It goes away.
You'll see someday.
How your sadness
is madness.

It's your doing.
So stop stewing
in your own juice.
It's no use.
Just let go
of those dead old
issues
that push you
around
and down
to the ground
in sorrow.
There is a tomorrow.
Let it be.
Come with me.
We are free.

11/25/2003
The Student

GLASS STONES

I broke out
I broke free
and now I've confused myself.
I have a house
I cannot see
a place where I abused the health
of the forest for the trees.
I thought I loved
but I was proved wrong.
When pleasure's peace dove
sang me her song,
the passion left
my heart sore,
in the house that would never be a home
on its own.

12/26/2005
The Occidental

HOUSEKEEPING

Why do I try to be stable?
As if personality is set in stone
like the big brick walls we build
all they do is keep up alone.
It's change that brings us closer to love
and love is what creates home
not stability
or big brick buildings.
Change, love, home.

7/29/2011
Walls

RETURNING TO WHOLENESS

It's dark here in This Place
in this corner of my heart.
I've been denying its existence,
pretending not to know.
I've let this corner alone,
I haven't been here in so long.
I hoped maybe with neglect,
this place would simply be gone.
I let love shine in my heart
to prove that it ceased to exist.
In that bright light of Truth I saw,
quite the opposite.
There, in juxtaposition to Love
to the joy that encompasses my heart,
after all the pain and angers gone,
This Place is my scar.
It still hurts to come here.
But now I come without fear.
The mirror is clear.
The darkness
Is at rest.
I know the grace
within This Place
My Soul
is Whole.

2/18/2011
Walls

FREEDOM

Freedom is not a logical concept
a law, a right, a system.
Freedom is a Gift we must accept.
It starts in our dreams.
It grows from within.
So many prisons
we have built
of shame and guilt
unforgiven sins.
Against our own truth.
our own sense of self.
At the bottom of the well
we face our own hell
that only we could make
from our own fear and pain.
But once we look the demon in the eye,
own it and trust it and give it space to cry,
we give our dream the tools to survive.
We grow with our dreams as they blossom and
        thrive.
We fuse our will and our love into one.
We believe and we finally become
Freedom.

6/4/2014
Back Home Again

WHAT TO WRITE

The time has come
that the poet's prose
is reduced to relations of endless injustice.
When the Divine
cannot rhyme
for the sake of sounding childish.
As the Fire
smokes you higher
in the name of what is truest.
But the climb
is in your mind
realizing that you're clueless.
At the end
we must be friends
because all things change
and rearrange
and seal
and heal
with time.

4/14/2002
The Stowaway

POETRY

The prose that you know
from inside to out
so well that you dwell
in the words that you shout.
They frame your brain
like it's hanging on a wall
but meaning is secondary
to the feeling of it all.
So then,
what are words but shirts,
we can take off and put on,
but the stains remain the same,
because we eat the same shit all day long.
And the meaning we are gleaning
will stay the same too.
Because prose can change like clothes,
but you will still be you.

12/11/2003
Germany

INSPIRATION

spins in a circle
from one to another
the muses mother
those great themes
that inspire dreams
and sweet new lovers
to sing those ancient stories
into fresh existence
like the blossoms of spring flowers
with the sun's persistence.

6/17/2011
Walls

HEART BEAT

Boom Boom
I light my heart on fire
now in sight of my desire
burning bright this funeral pyre
I lay that love to rest.
The Path in front of me to choose
or bask in sunny mountain views
until at last I do conclude
and do as I find best.
Boom Boom
A stronger beat returns
A longer heat heart fire burn
A song for my heart to remember learn
because I know it's true.
One love, one life, one destiny.
My dream of not strife will come to be.
My brother, my sister, I live in peace.
And I want to share it with you.

6/6/2003
The Stowaway

MELODY

swam in one ear
and out the other
before I even noticed
I was listening
I heard
the balancing
changes in frequencies
resonating
against my ear drum
as I hum

8/5/2010
The Night Pages

DREAM

That special place between
reality and possibility
steeped in memory
like strong black tea
and fresh honey.
See how it tastes
when daylight breaks
and you want to hang on
to a half heard idea of a maybe song
lingering on your brain's tongue
before you open your eyes.

inspired by 'Sandman' by Neil Gaiman

7/29/2011
Walls

I JUMPED

not so gracefully
into the void.
I was afraid
for the first few moments
but then it became comforting.
The lack
became peace.

7/10/2010
The Night Pages

NIGHT TRAIN

The sound of the train whistle
wafting through the night
rattled around in my hollow body
like the wind in the trees,
whispering in my ear
echoing my loneliness,
bouncing off my thoughts
until they've all been shattered
against the hard inside of my skull.
I reach a moment of peace
no longer yearning,
accepting of my own void
after the jump.
Solitude.

8/18/2010
The Night Pages

DAWN

at the edge of two lives,
two selves,
she who was
and she who will be.
Tomorrow is not quite here,
limbo,
the in between.
I've been here before
as a little girl.
I guess I missed it,
because I keep coming back.

4/20/2018
New Baby

BOAT OF WEEDS

On hope
I float
what a little boat.
This earth
with it's wide gerth
can be
floating free
gloating it seems,
over flowing with dreams.
What a mind blowing scene!
Glowing green
teeming with life seeds
growing like weeds.

1/7/2004
The Student

*

Sometimes when a person walks along their path
they have a good reason to stop.
Maybe a flower in a sunlight bath
exalted from bottom to top.
Reflection ensues on a person's own life.
A sweet inner peace can be born.
So real and so deep
starting from the inside
showing all of the masks you have worn.

2/10/2003
Germany

LAZY DAY

After a lifetime of escaping:
Books, daydreams, hallucinations.
Maybe the story i want
Is my own.
This moment right here.
Written on the breeze in the branches.
Emotion gets lost in the hum of the city
Just outside my garden.
I consider sprawling like the cat
In the late evening warmth,
But my body doesn't really lay flat like that.
My butt would fall asleep.
While I'm lazing about,
Staring at the swaying grasses, the dead roses and the
    bright blue wild flowers.

7/10/2020
Emails

ONE HEART

I read your story
about orange blossoms
and the young doctor who died.
Tears pooled in the corners of my eyes
until they ran down my cheeks.
I looked up into the spring
new green on the trees
and the tears running down my face
met over my naked heart
and became one stream
of sorrow
of beauty
of Love.

5/10/2020
Tiger Stripes and Leopard Spots

WHITE SPACE

I close my eyes and stand at the foot of the biggest
    boldest words.
They grow and grow.
Mountainous words.
So big.
So much.
Intention, meaning, imposing on me.
You must understand!
In between the letters
the space is inviting.
From here the words mean nothing.
I can rest.
Not trying to understand.
I don't know.
My comfort.

1/9/2019 Wednesday
Emails

THINKING

The sky did its best impression of winter
turning murky blue grey just before sunrise.
I caught my mind drifting back to sleep
regardless of the state of my eyes.
Maybe when your heart is wide open
reflection is imperative.
Like the white trim of the neighbor's windows
love shines back through the dark what you give
hinting at shapes in the morning twilight,
true light of spirit,
recollecting.

9/30/2010
The Night Pages

STILL FEELING

The first wave of stillness is emotion.
Raw, undefined, the wild ocean.
It does not need a reason, or a name.

Fear, love, sad, happy are just labels, small.
The feeling just is, and you feel it All.
This emotion is bigger than you.

It's hard not to give it a cause.
Not to use it to do, to really just pause.
To feel so much, so deeply, then let it go.

on the koan 'No'

7/1/2016
The Stormlers Sprout

NEW OR NOT?

There was a me
who was young wild and free,
who did things out of order
just to see if it mattered,
who tip-toe Stomped
to surprise the unwitting,
who got easily lost,
she was hard and not kidding.

She's still there
somewhere
buried in curls of hair
that clog the drain.

She grew.

She changed.

Now I laugh harder and longer
I love deeper and stronger.
I don't push buttons,
I push Truth,
like a tree full of fruit.
Let's eat our fill
and tell some more tales

about Love and laughter
and live happily ever after.

for my birthday

8/3/2017
New Baby

Spirit

TIP TOE STOMP

The MoonCat sneaks
giggling away the darkened streets.
Blue eyes flashing
mischievous grin crashing
the party of your expectations.
Inviting love creations!
Come dance on the table
and invent wild fables
that all end in dreams
and cookies and cream
And more love than anyone could ever ignore
It is what it was and will be before.

11/15/2010
Walls

MOONCAT

Sneaking by
like a cat in the night.
You won't even notice
as I steal your heart.
Just a little smile
at just the right time.
You won't even notice
I've made my mark,
Till you catch yourself humming a tune to the moon
and wishing on all of the stars.

2/19/2012
Butterfly

CAUGHT IN THE ACT

I was watching today
letting time slip away
trying to catch myself in the act.
I threw my head back and surrendered to laugh
at the completely ridiculous humanity of myself
my attachments to ideas of goodness or wealth.
I spent so many years trying to feel free
realizing now all I had to do was Be Me.
Society sees me comin' a mile away.
Stealth has never been my strong suit.
I think I like it better that way
to live with abandon and passion, my Truth,
giving my heart and my love as I go
in service, in wisdom to the cycle of needs.
Helping the seeds of the Universe grow,
the Universe, in turn, helping to grow me.

3/23/2011
Walls

149

SOURCE

Sometimes wonder lines my life runway
with lights during the day
when I'm not looking,
like it's cooking
up kinds of signs
to send me
when I'm not ready,
when I'm waiting
for something else to happen,
it appears
searing my eyes with its bright light,
shining in the night like a beacon
of pure energy
divine.

1/10/2004
The Student

THE NEW YEAR

Came in dripping
still tipsy
drunk on revelation
consecrating the passage
with its warm sticky love juice.
We lapped it up
with our spongey tongues
and reveled
in sweet blessed passion
offering our bodies
including heart and mind
as sacrament to consume
in honor of the times.

1/1/2011
Walls

BELIEVE

Burning candle
Light my fire
Bright Full Moon
Proper attire.
Naked as the day I was born.

Set the intention
Open heart mind
Inhabit the body
Let go of pride.
This moment is Blessed by the Gods and the Norn.

Our bodies twinkle
Stars in the night
Love kindles Magic
Prayer transcends Time.
Let's dance until our Souls are worn.

7/21/2014
Back Home Again

PROOF

I offered my heart to the Goddess
and she generously blessed me!
She showed me the Path
and opened your heart to me.
I never knew a love like this
I couldn't imagine a way to exist
so sweetly intertwined
with someone so divine
a constant reminder of the beauty of life
releasing me from worry and everyday strife
I am loved.
So are you.
The Divine exists within.
We are Proof!

2/1/2011
Walls

ARTISTS PRAYER

Space time continuum drift
allowing the seams to split
devotion includes emotion
and we all share the gift.
Thoughts like lilies
float down the stream of consciousness.
Dreams expertly express
the newness of release.
The beauty of the void
the moment is ceaseless,
as we rise above the droid
the functionality
purpose takes a vacation
we open to the Goddess
and invite creation.

December 2009
The Night Pages

WATER

Water is flowing across the land
turning the rocks into gravel and sand.
Refreshing the mountains with its cold.
Feeding the trees and are ever-growing old.
We drink from the gush
constantly surrounding us.
More than we living can ever understand,
the river flows on
the moment is gone
and it slips through the fingers of our hand.

FIRE

Flicker flame dancing
a whirling red romancing
of our human sense of spirit
we can feel it, see it, hear it.
And it absorbs us in it all.
And we bask there in its halls.
So fickle and precarious,
and so we would take care for us,
that remembrance of the burn
that is the fire's turn

and telling love to be
be inspired again within me.

6/20/2002
The Stowaway

TIGER LOVE

I'm hungry again.
My heart is racing.
I want something outside myself
to tell me it will be ok.
So many unknowns this week.
Next week there will be more.
I don't have to close my eyes
to see the Tiger in my heart.
Patience, she says.
Fear turns vulnerability into danger.
So be strong.
Be soft and fierce.
Be Love.

5/24/2020
Tiger Stripes and Leopard Spots

SPIDER PROTECTION

I was scared last night.
Grandmother Spider came and sat on my house.
Her giant furry legs dangling over the windows
as webbing crept down the walls.
She smiled, that knowing mischief smile,
and I knew we were safe,
from the dark eyed predators
gnashing their teeth
at the gate.

8/10/2017 Thursday
New Baby

GODDESS IN THE LIGHTNING

Thunder Rolls and shakes the roof.
I cried out to the Goddess,
Trust Is So Hard!
Then don't.
She said.
I'll carry you anyway.
Lightning cracked.
I saw her silhouette.
Giant Spider crouching over my house.
Your tears are my worship.
Your body has been my temple.
You are me as much as I am You.

8/29/2019 Thursday
Emails

GIANT SNAKE GODDESS

rose up over me.
She coiled around me
strong, thick, black and tan shimmying.
Her fangs went all the way through my neck
as she bit.
Venom coursed through my veins.
Numbness.
My legs, my arms, my face. Gone.
My womb, my heart, all that remains.
I became her.
Her eyes took over my face.
Writhing slowly, I am surrounded
in a swirling mass of snakes.
I am Mother.
I am the end and the beginning.
A thousand arms.
A thousand children
all of them mine.
Transform yourself.
Shed your Life.
Become, Priestess.
Become.

9/7/2020 Monday Night
Tiger Stripes and Leopard Spots

THE CHESHIRE MOON

grew into a mandarin orange slice.
Peeking through the fat leaved trees
in the late summer breeze,
threatening to Autumn.
I smiled back.
Dusk became night
and the stars sent us all to bed
with mischief cat dreams for a snack.

8/28/2017
New Baby

TRANSFORMATION OF NIGHT

The Darkness
Reminds me to slow down.
There's no running at night unless you're drunk on
    love or booze or fear.
I take my steps a little more carefully.
As my eyes adjust, I become more bold,
But I never break with keeping one foot on the
    ground.

The Moon
Reminds me to love.
She softens the edges of daytime.
Throws sexy shadows and lovely shimmer on bodies
    and faces.
I see myself and my love and my heart opens,
My inner critic will return, but moonlight kissed
    memories will sweeten her.

The Fog
Reminds me to dream.
Everything and Nothing blend into possibility.
My eyes look for fairies and ghosts and my heart
    skips a beat.
I cling to your arm and my imagination drifts.
The rules of reality bend and doors to different
    futures open and close.

11/18/2019
Emails

NEW CLEANSING

Walking down the alley
in between the streets
we meet
we hug and kiss
and look into eachother's eyes
there's the sky
reflecting my mood like always
calming at best
I rest.
You understand the moment
all for what it's worth.
My birth.
Reborn under the morning overcast
the clouds are in my palm.
I am calm.
You join me in child's pose
head to cement releasing my pain,
it rains.

6/6/2003
The Stowaway

THE DEEP

Into the deep
the wise woman walked
searching for a place of grace
in the darkness
under the belly of man
where ego falls
and desire is an illusion
she found the crossroads
of time and love
with guides by her side
she transformed
she opened her heart to the world as it was
and opened her mind to the world as it will be
and became a conduit for the world as it is
she prayed
for peace
happiness
compassion
and understanding

4/5/2014
Back Home Again

MORRIGAN'S CALL

Child, you are mine.
You always have been.
We have looked in the eyes of the greatest warriors
as their light faded.
We know their legacy.
We wrote their prophecy.
You held the pen,
together we wrote the words,
over the bloodied battlefields,
encircled by our mighty black birds.

8/28/2020
Tiger Stripes and Leopard Spots

TIDE

Come here
where the sand is made
millennia of mountains
slowly fade
where birds die
in winds too high
for them
only the ocean
was meant to survive
in this place
of change
the day after death
while the channels are open
to say our goodbyes
to close our eyes
and honor the end
before life again
a funeral for dreams
dressed in feathers and sand
barnacles and foam
and the churning edge of the sea.

9/15/2014
Back Home Again

OLD FRIEND

Death is a dear old friend of mine.
Like most old friends I've seen different sides.
Once he came to me tall and imposing.
Clock chimes tolling, midnight closing.
Telling me nothing I can do matters.
Wild dark cape, bones and tatters.
Floating in the moonlight.
Scary that night.

One time Death was a little girl.
Ash dusty face and wild tangled curls.
That night she looked like me when I cry.
Crouched and suspicious with wet dark eyes.
She brought me to the resting bones of my cat.
She knew exactly where they were at.
In the cemetery of guides,
who were once by our sides.

She knitted his thin bones into my muscles.
She taught me how to sit up and look just so.
She taught me to stalk and saunter and purr.
And I swear for a moment I could feel his fur.
Over my skin.
I was almost him.

And she told me there,
under the stars between layers,

that he is part of me now.
Teaching me how.
To be a fine black feline.
Dapper and divine.
Death is an old friend of mine.

For Bruce

2016

Nature

SEASON TIME LOVE

Walking dusty licks of sand.
Holding grains of time in hand.
Floating, whirling, spinning round.
Above, below, into the ground.
While this love ignites such fires
as set the Gods unto desire.
For all the world has yet to see
that all along its love was me,
And as the clouds above did cross
below the earth was laced with frost,
and lakes of ice were frozen through
and all the world was ready to renew
its vows of spring and summer and fall.
Winter is not so bad at all.
Once viewed through the eternal hourglass
as time of present, future and past,
Nothing to say, but smile and nod,
at the morning sun, burning the fog.
The seasons change
and the reasons remain
for ancient is this love of mine,
the seasons eternal love of time.

12/20/2001
The Travel Book

BUTTERFLY

Dancing with the breeze,
Kissing the flowers and leaves.
Painting the sunlight with wings.
The sunlight kisses my cheeks with color.
I dance with my love in the shade
and the butterflies play music to our eyes.

7/6/2018 *Friday*
Emails

WATER

pouring
spilling dropping
filling tipping
over the edge of my heart cup
so full of love
we shared
and tears we shed
the ocean
of emotion
opens in my soul
come float
across the waves
let go of time and space

11/21/2014
Moving Away

*

Fresh morning breeze
rustling the trees
green in the leaves
mottles the sunlight.
Gentle rebirth
grounded in the earth
springing from self worth
after the dark night.
Trust in each moment
love shine divine sent
the leaves know what you meant
and the breeze makes it alright.

8/13/2014
Back Home Again

SEASONS

Summer is different this year,
cooler, calmer, more collected.
Maybe we're not quite there yet,
to the melt,
to the sweet hot sweat
on the edge of wet.
The breeze still lingers
and spring licks her fingers...

6/17/2011
Walls

SUMMER

I know…
Life is like a dance!
Oh Yeah.
Fanciful colors
smothering you
with every move.
This creation
of sensation,
one expression
can unfold
entire world
before your nose
Breathe deep.
Sweet heat
of excitement,
it grows.

Summer 2004
The Pod

*

Slow flowing river
step into the stream
of the daydream
with a sigh and a shiver.

Refreshing and cool
in the heat of the day
and the logical fray
of the mind as a tool.

Let your heart explore
story images flow free
floating gently towards the sea
or resting on the shore.

8/13/2014
Back Home Again

MY FAVORITE THINGS

I love long skinny branches
with leaves that grow in pairs,
and little girls who giggle
with flowers in their hair,
and that moment when the clouds part
and sunshine streaks the sky,
or a big fat yellow moon
rising over the treetops at night.
A smile from someone who knows you too well,
hugs from a new friend.
Delicious soup on a cold day,
and stories that never end.

Fall 2016
Emails

ALMOST FALL

Late summer, morning rain
washes the smell of wood fire smoke out of my nose.
Old love songs on the radio.
Cream swirling in my coffee.
Tangled hair and overgrown vines,
inviting scratchy unshaven kisses.
Fall unfolding under our noses.

Thursday August 30th, 2018
Jonny Scribbles

TWO FIRES

I never saw the fire
I didn't even see the smoke
but it made it so I could not stay.
Everything got hazy
 the sun turned angry
a matte red orb of heat.

We lost everything.
Except my instruments and my passport.
Except the rivers and the animals that could run.

Its just stuff.
The forest will grow back.
But neither will ever be replaced.

9/3/2014
New Baby

ALL AT ONCE

Night.
Snow.
The edge of town.

Baby crying.
Wolf howling.
A single siren on the highway.

He woke up in pain.
I am dreaming.
Someone's house is on fire.

My fear.
My love.
Nature.

2/24/2018
New Baby

MANIFEST RAIN DESTINY

The rain falls
softer than the breath of my lover.
Still man's machines
find a way to make noise with it.
Even before dawn
wakes the man,
we who still hear the forest,
who remember the importance of rain,
are reminded of man's destructive progress.
The Rain will wash that away too,
in time.

10/10/2012
Butterfly

NW LOVE

Once in a while love means letting go.
Snow.
Every great love comes with its fair share of pain.
Rain.
Good love has some passion and sexy sizzle.
Drizzle.
But deep true love is built to last.
Overcast.

12/22/2018 Saturday
Emails

THE STARS OF FALL

Look Up.
Let the thin bare branches
melt into the sky.
Focus on the last remnants of leaves
flickering in the reflected firelight.
The stars are bigger, brighter.
Shining steady through the gaps.
Twinkling as the wind rustles.
The smoke and the tree and the night
gently shifting.
Swirling slowly.
The stars and the leaves and the dark
harmony of elements.
Autumn night serenity.

11/24/2013
Back Home Again

LITTLE NW WINTER THINGS

Sparkles and stars,
eyes and ornaments,
big smiles with two tiny teeth,
droplets of rain glittering in the morning sun,
wisps of fog on the mountain,
cat hair on my black shirt,
baby toes and kitty noses,
Pine needles and purrs.

12/14/2017
Invite to Solstice

*

dusk in the deep forest
heavy rains turn the sky grey blue
the trees look like they're under water
sagging in the downpour
floating like kelp
through the spring storm

5/15/2017
New Baby

TREES

Deep forest green
carpets my heart
sitting on the edge
looking into the reflection
which is the void.
Feeling transformed.
Not wanting to linger
but unwilling to leave.
It's hard to remember
we are never alone.

9/4/2010
The Night Pages

Sex

SUMMER OF YES

Summer came in hot and sweaty,
Ready.
Not about to wait
for your dreams
and your fantasy scenes.
Flowers like towers
on long sexy greens.
She says Bless
to the mess.
Let's play today!
Without reality all in the way.
In the Heat.
And the Sweat.
And the Yes.

5/30/2014
Back Home Again

HOT

The heat came
and sank its teeth into my bones
it shook its head
and with it my hips
caught in the grip
of summer's passion

Summer 2010
The Night Pages

JUICY

Unsure of my willingness to participate
I tripped
and slipped down onto
the sultry wet tongue of summer
still sticky with blackberry juice
dripping together
on the crisp linen sheets

Summer 2010
The Night Pages

CLEAN SHEET DAY

clean sheets
of paper on my bed
starched to perfection
waiting to be
ruffled with seduction
sex outside the covers
where I can see your naked ass
crumpling my pages
in the reflective glass

Summer 2011
Loose Leaf

SOFT

Our bodies pressed
together
rarely exposed skin
gently expanding
to the touch
the vulnerability
of relaxing
letting ourselves be
unfiltered, unfettered
honest
generating warmth
embracing.

for Tim, the best snuggler

1/26/2015
The Stormlers Sprout

SENSUAL REACTION

I can still smell you
hours after you've left my room.
I can feel the air vibrating,
my skin starts to tingle,
standing close to you.
Finding myself shy
in your eyes.
Scared but hopeful,
your words tumble
through my being,
picking up meaning
as they roll around my heart.

8/21/2010
The Night Pages

KISS

Your lips blanket my tongue
twisting into a dance of wetness
slipping, squishing, sucking
skin taste tingling deliciousness
tickling my awareness
with hints of pheromones
and sticky sweet notes
leftover from the mornings breakfast
of love and pancakes
hot off the griddle
ready to melt in your mouth!

11/08/2010
Walls

*

Just one kiss
is all it takes
it breaks
and shakes
inside my soul
divide my whole
into bliss bits
your hands on my hips.
Sprinkle on
wrinkles in
time
forever divine
your lips pressed to mine.
Touch my neck
or my cheek
nothing left
I can't speak.
So full
of pleasure
my bowl
of treasure
is your soul
in a breath
in the depths
of your kiss.

8/31/2014
Back Home Again

*

Firm and juicy
you grew on me.
I didn't like it at first
but what's worse?
I couldn't look away.
I wanted to stay.
I wanted to know for sure.
Feel the pure raging sensation course through.
till I knew.
This is it.
This is Bliss.

5/30/2014
Back Home Again

ENGINES OF LOVE

Turning
churning
burning away
the debris of the mundane.
Daily life
it's a crisis
of healing
and feeling
I'm still reeling
with the bigness
the stress
of it all
but I'm Blessed
as I fall.
Don't question the awe
just caress
and surrender
remember
to make love
with your soul
use your hips
as we roll
put your lips
on my throat
feed the bliss

with each kiss.
Grow
slow.

8/2/2014
Back Home Again

PLAY

I can't ignore it
the smell of your sweat
deep like the forest
and sweeter yet.
One dance with you
and my brain is soaked through
from all of my senses.
I've dropped my defenses.
Pretenses melt.
Intentions are felt.
No need for words
this moment is pure.
Just gentle emotion
and bodies in motion
letting go
in the flow
and the sway
let's play.

8/3/2014
Back Home Again

Love

OPEN

to knowing.
Stop hoping.
Believe.
Receive
your needs.
Trust
in Love.
Lust
is not enough.
Fires
of desire
can fade,
be unmade.
The Ocean
is endless
it holds the stars
and all that you are.
Everything that is, was and will be
comes back to rest in the sea
in the heart
in me.

9/20/2014
Back Home Again

SUNRISE

After a strange dream
of past lovers
having bread and tea.
French bistro view
softens the spiked skyline.
Bittersweet memories
of a harsher time.
Hope on the horizon.
Suffering every day.

8/29/2019
Emails

LOVE LIKE A TREE

Your Love is a Forest
not a Lone Pine
don't force it
let your heart fly.

You love like we do
connected at the roots
to many others
creating the support structure
for life of all kinds.

Where you grow so close together
that each breath is a kiss
every lean an embrace
every new leaf a wish.

Set your heart free.
Love like a Tree.

8/22/2014
Back Home Again

REFLECTING ON YOU IN ME

I feel you so deep.
In places I forgot how to feel,
your heart beats.
Soft solid rhythm so real
undeniable
gently penetrating, but freeing.
So Reliable,
slowly permeating my being.
Showing me to myself
in a way I could never have seen.
New meaning to heath,
allowing me to come clean.
Clearing a space
for my heart to start anew.
The smile on your face
reflecting me in you.

11/15/2010
Walls

*

Your strong arms
enfold my heart.
Your steady gaze
melts my fear.
Your hands unlock secrets
in my skin.
My soul
invites you in.

Stay near.
Keep me warm.
Hold my hand.

Together
we'll weather
the roots of our plan.

Grow into
each other,
Partners. Lovers.

6/14/2015
Moving Away

THE SHADY GROVE

I watched you turn on the light,
even though the sun was out.
In our Shady Grove, even at high noon
there's always a little darkness about,
snuggling into the corners
like the smile on your mouth
reassuring me gently
in my lonely hour of doubt
that everything is ok
no matter what time of day.

for Zack Tigert

7/29/2011
Walls

*

In a rumpled swirl
of blankets and sheets,
my love sleeps.
His thinking mind
finally quieting,
after the day's anxieties.
Drifting on the dream tides.
I hope they are gentle.
Rest for the next day's mental ride.
So many ideas,
considerations,
clamoring for the waking time.
May the early morning hours
prove fruitfully empty.

for Tim

6/14/2015
Moving Away

ONE LOVING THOUGHT

pursued by another.
A Lover.
I try
smiling.
My reflect
connects
with the last one
Love
so deep.
Head to feet
steeped
in the glory
this morning
of knowing
by showing
my weakness
I am blessed
with reciprocation.
An application
of the theory
of the weary.
When you are tired,
Keep On.

5/5/2004
The Pod

HARD LOVE

separation
as essential
for revelation
subsequential
realization
of the downfall
of the world
curled
around your every word
I heard it right
tonight
I'm sure
of what I endure
to be with you
your true
and relentless love
replenishes
every moment of mine
I know time is no obstacle
in my course
of worse
circumstances
and clumsy dances
with fake lights
in the awake nights
I turn over
and by my shoulder

I feel your breath
your depth

Fall 2004
The Lost Pages

DON'T CRY, JUST DREAM

Soft and warm
supportive.
My safe place
to bury my face.
Nuzzle in
after a long day.
There's always one long chest hair
that tickles my nose.
But I have the best dreams
with your shoulder as my pillow.

11/30/2012
Butterfly

HEART HAMMER

Acute wooden triangle
spike of doubt
wedged in your heart.
Each word out of my mouth,
another blow with a 9 pound hammer.
Splitting your Trust.
We need the Whole Truth.
I can't be honest without hurting you.
Omission leaves slivers in our tender love.
This is why I cut and run.
So I don't splinter.
A clean break
heals faster.

1/21/2013
Butterfly

AIR MEN

Magnificent wounded bird,
champion of flight,
grounded.
Come float in my ocean.
Let my salt
clean your cuts
until they bleed red.
Heal at the source
cradled in my waves
supported by current.
Flowing,
let yourself drift.
I will deposit you,
safely on a better shore,
ready to fly again.

9/28/2014
Back Home Again

RIPPED

We were broken people.
Who made a broken thing together.
Held together and pulled apart
by attachment to our former selves.
Each step forward ripping into our hearts
as we tried to drag the past with us,
instead of letting go,
and letting ourselves grow.

for Rob

3/22/2013
Butterfly

MIXED HEART MESSAGES

listing
twisting
intentions
into new inventions
retention prevention
shifting dimensions
until I'm unsure
of the Truth anymore.

My own heart
foreign object
I lost it
somewhere
under a chair?
as a dare
to my wild hare Self.

When I looked in your eyes
my smile went wide
expanded my mind
my plans grew wings to fly
and there they go
right out the window.

7/25/2014
Back Home Again

NOT IN LOVE

The early morning chill
of not quite fall
intensifies the color spray of sunrise,
reflecting my heart.
As I recall your smile
dazzling for a moment
but distant.
My body tells me I'm cold.
I feel my blood slowing.
But my mind is caught
replaying the same memory.
Finally, me heart weeps.
My soul translates for my feet:
Let's go home.

9/9/2010
The Night Pages

AT THE TRAIN CROSSING

The train came.
I was caught on one side of the tracks.
My love was not with me,
so I cried.
I knew the train would pass,
but for a sweet moment,
I was alone at the crossing.
Allowed to feel.
To grieve the loss that the mind knows is fleeting,
but the heart feels anyway.
The train cars crush by.
Tears gush forth.
I wail.
Safe in the cacophony of the train.
I lose my voice to sobbing.
The caboose chugs by with an extra clanging bell.
As the bars lift,
signaling my bodily safety,
my heart quiets.
My mind takes over.
I know my love will return.
I am thankful for the safety of the
Train Crossing.
Allowing my heart the safety
to feel pain.

3/14/2014
Back Home Again

277

LOVE IN THE SEASON OF UNCERTAINTY

Nothing is for sure you say.
Not ever.
True.
Everything is subject to change.
Always.
True.
But I don't feel afraid.
Because we're together.
So, if everything changes.
Will I?
Will you?

12/10/2019
Emails

LETTING YOU DRIVE

I still want to know where I'm going
even though I may never get there.
Somehow having an idea, a purpose
makes discomfort easier to bear.
It's so much easier to love the journey
knowing it will end.
Every journey is unique,
we can never do This, again.
So pick a place and a time
and I promise we'll get there
it's not my fault, I might be lying,
but I know you love me anywhere.

7/29/2011
Walls

OUR LOVE IS MY TEMPLE

There's a beautiful temple in my heart
that you and I built
brick by brick
kiss by kiss.
It holds my dreams.
Our Family.
Our Home.
It generates magic
that makes the best life.

for Tim

8/26/2017
New Baby

Family

FAMILY

Such a big word
to be heard
in one sitting
knitting
a web so fitting.
No kidding.
It's important to me
not to be
just a face
in a place
in a sea
of people around
surrounding.
You ground me
for this fantasy
that comes to be
my reality
after a while.
I always smile
to think
that even at the brink
the frayed
and filleted
pieces of my heart
won't fall apart
because of you,
it's true.

These people that I love
that I think of
when I'm far
from any part
of what we together
have endeavored
to maintain
it remains.

Regardless
of our stress
of what type
of hype
this life
just might
be giving us
I trust
that you are there
that you care
because I do
and that's true.
No lies
I will die
with this love still.
My will
is so
that even though
we may
stray
someday
we come back
to family.
You see
what I mean?

In my eyes
when I try
to explain
beauty on this earth
there's a nerve
to be touched there
that we share
in this
bliss.
My family

Ever changing
but still the same
no shame.
Some battles
some rattles
some shattered hearts
we've played the parts.
At the end of it all
I stand tall
not proud
not allowed
to shout out loud
who I am
and where I stand
cause wherever I land
there's an open hand
and a heart full
and that pull
on my life
in any type
of situation
the implications
are huge

from my view.
I love you.
There's nothing I can do.
My heart's true
and real home
while I roam
is where?
There.
Where you are
however far
under whatever star.
You can never be
lost to me
My family.

11/25/2003
The Student

FOR DAD

The love of a father
who taught her
his daughter
to love the others
as brothers
each other,
but also stand alone
on her own
two feet
on that street
that she wanders down,
not to frown
not to fear
for love is always near
if you we'll lend an ear
just open your eyes
sometimes
and the things you will find
are wonderful
like a heart full
of love.

for my dad's birthday

04/23/2005
Paperback

291

FOR MOM

I have been very small
in your arms
you've seen all
of my heart
that there is to see
I believe.
You bathed me.
You've seen all my parts
all my false starts
the photo finishes
you were there for the beginning of it.
As I look back
I laugh
and I know you
are laughing too.
You held my Self
when I was scared.
I tell myself
when you're not there,
that you're not far
under the same stars,
somewhere.
I carry
that with me,
I do,

my love for you,
and inspiration above all others.
My mother.

for my mom's birthday

05/15/2005
Paperback

FAR FROM HOME

Loneliness struck my heart
this morning at 1:30am
I watched home depart
on the first bus
the day after Christmas.
So I cried
for lack of options.
Why?
I don't really understand myself.
I hid in my blankets
my last refuge of mental health.
Sleep.
I wake.
I weep.
So far away from the world where I began
that I figured I'd grow into.
Somewhere I lost the plan,
the blueprint I had
for life,
the one she gave me first.
I miss her.
Plan or not,
distance
can never sever
the connection between us,
it is forever.

12/26/2005
The Occidental

WALLS

the boundaries
the limits we set
on ourselves
on our heart
to protect us from falling apart
but it's a false sense of security
all it does is keep you from me
deny the flow
of friendship and love
walls create corners
against which we shove
or worse
we force
our hearts into them
to hide our fear
from our friends.

for the Walls Notebook

6/17/2011
Walls

*

You speak to me openly
vulnerable, questioning
asking for the connection
open access to the collection
of wisdom humanity has assembled in my knowing.
And I care
so I will always meet you there
and every time
I'm reminded
of my own pleas for help.
A reflection of my soul
in the experience of one I know.
My comrade, teacher, friend of heart.

for George Moore

7/13/2011
Walls

FOR STEVY

Glory
shines so brightly sometimes.
We are blinded
by blacklights
and neon duct tape
and dancing ultra shimmer fabric.
Crackle pop static
comes over the air waves
as we bravely
walk away
from our dreams
those first star wishes
falling around our ears
our fears
force open the next door
we're not choosing anymore
we let the choice be made for us
out of trust?
no, out of weakness.
To be strong
we must first remember
to choose
for ourselves
whichever path,
only then do we become
the heroes we dream of.

for Vy, my childhood best friend

Loose Leaf

NATURAL LOVE

Wandering Rainbows, drifting in and out of my life,
    turn my head.
I smile, so does she, and we walk together instead.
And what a beautiful walk! In the trees, in the forest.
We walked for miles and the noise of the world
    ingored us.
She loved me, I loved her.
She loves me, I love her.
She will love me, I will love her.
The sunset is a rise when we share everything,
the earth below our feet stirs when she sings.
And I hear it, then I feel it, then of course, I dance
    to it.
Then the trees dance too, because everyone loves to
    do it.
And she wanders, and I wander
and we get through it.
So I wonder, she wonders too,
but we both knew it.
And we know, will know,
because it is us, and we love,
because we are love.

for Melissa Allen, my Cookie

6/22/2003
The Stowaway

THE TRUEST CIRCLE

being a woman
is not always easy
so let us dance the night away
bask in the rays
that friendship provides us
the midnight path
back from the hot springs at dusk
is still lit with love
as we sit in this cove
and remind each other
we are not brothers
we are greater
we are sisters
 we are makers
of dreams and reality
it seems unending
unbeginning
the circle of friendships love

for Ursala

7/12/2006
Back in the USA

BELOVED

The perpetual motion of my heart
strays to my feet
keeping the beat.
While my heart wanders
the connections made
while it's out at play
are never squandered,
they are cherished.
Love is my treasure.
You are a jewel.

for my best friend Jess

7/30/2010
The Night Pages

REMIND ME OF MYSELF

Reflecting with you
reminded me of my Truth.
The Gift of sight
through another's eyes.
Father sky
looked back at me
pouring me a cup of tea
listening to my story
remembering the glory
of life in its complexity.
Returning with me to serenity.
Back to peace in Love again.
Thank you, my friend.

for my friend Bobbie

3/13/2011
Walls

THE POND

splash!
You jumped in
before you knew how to swim
it was slippery and cold
you tried everything you know
to stay afloat
without a boat
to breathe.
You became part of the sea
of people who tried
who survive
without getting churned under
by other people's blunders
who learned to fish
just loosen your grip
and let reality
flow free.

for my brother Bron

6/17/2011
Walls

INSPIRATION

You said something once,
in passing,
that touched my heart.
I cherish those words.
I've built ten stories
to give them more meaning,
but the stories don't matter.
What matters is the feeling.
Seen and honored,
by your casual witnessing.
Those who have come
through the fire,
are not startled by
the flame.

for Barry Graham

12/17/2015
The Stormlers Sprout

313

FRIENDS FROM BEFORE

I saw you first
on accident,
a glimpse into your soul
before it was ready
for public scrutiny,
when doubt was allowed
and fear.
I kissed your tears
in those dark moments.
We held hands
in the shadowy corners,
when hope was foolish,
and I would do it again.

for Katsura Balanza

12/17/2015
The Stormlers Sprout

FATHERHOOD

Did you come here to cry?
I looked at him
and asked with my eyes
that question, too proud
to be asked aloud.
He wept.
Not with tears,
with underlying tones.
The guilt
the doubt,
causing fresh wrinkles
in his beautiful young skin.
'She'll be fine'
The one thing he really wants to hear.
No longer worries for himself,
his greatest fear,
for this father,
is his daughter.

for Mark

Fall 2007
Back in the USA

THE DECISION

We talked serious and laughed and cried
we made the hard call
with our hearts in our hands.
The way was unsure.
It was time to close the door.

That future with you
would never come true,
even though I've seen us in my dreams.
Laughing together as you grew.

Now I'm in the foggy clearing,
ghosts of future doors
hanging just out of view.
The hardest part is the
Not Knowing.
I always felt like I knew
when the way was with You.

2/19/2020 Wednesday
Emails

319

WALKING TOWARDS BIRTH

My belly swells,
My child grows,
Fluttering and rolling
Against the inside of my skin.

I take a step deeper
Into the catacombs,
My cave of old wounds and bad habits,
and read the writing on the wall.

We're on our Paths
To meet at birth
And create each other.
A new life.

to my son Raven

11/19/2016
Emails

NEW BABY

My heart sings!
The song is for you.
You are my dream.
My dream come true.

Sweet bear baby,
I will hold you in my arms.
The way is open for you
To come through my heart.

2/25/2020
Emails

MOTHER'S LOVE

Watching you sleep
puts my heart at rest.
Your little half smile
for a dreaming split second
is magic for my tired spirit.

When you cry out in pain
it brings me to my knees.
I'd give my entire being
to give you peace.

The light in your eyes
when you smile,
is the highest high
and the deepest joy of my life.

I will always love you.

for my son

5/15/2017
New Baby

MOTHER HANDS

My mother's hands are scarred,
they are beautiful.
Her palms are deeply and shallowly lined.
When she takes off her rings
I can see where they go.
Her hands have grown into them.
Her fingers are knobby and muscular,
strong and capable.
They show their imperfections,
and it makes them more beautiful.

3/14/2014
Back Home Again

THE BEST VIEW

I know you like to look at trees,
so I make sure you can see them.
I don't mind looking at the dirty cat box,
or the harsh glinting sun.
I want you to see the best parts of life,
when you're in my arms, on my shoulder,
hugging my neck, relaxed against me.
I give you the best view.
May you always see the beautiful side of life.

for my son Jonagold

7/31/2017
New Baby

GROWING TOGETHER

A Muse came this winter
to live at our house.
I made her a cozy living room.
She brought me a shelf.
I gave her comfort.
She gave me freedom.
We let our dreams grow,
until they became inspirations.
Like soup on a cold day
simmering until the flavors blended together
to become something new.

12/30/2019
Tiger Stripes and Leopard Spots

THE END

I saw us die.
You go first.
I follow a few years after.
Wild grey sprouting from my head,
enough for both of us;
waning light on your bald crown.
Warm wool blankets and sunsets
are more important.
Two lifetimes,
one collection of memories.
Moments woven together,
finite basketry of notions and feelings,
carries us to the infinite edge
beyond life.

For my husband, Tim

2/1/2016
The Stormlers Sprout

CPSIA information can be obtained
at www.ICGtesting.com
Printed in the USA
BVHW030946090621
609091BV00004B/249